GREETINGS FROM

CALIFORNIA POST

For Grandma Jane and
Grandpa Wayne, and for
the Bibbs and Spences.

—JSS

Published by Familius™ LLC, www.familius.com

Familius books are available at special discounts for bulk purchases for sales promotions or
for family or corporate use. For more information, contact Premium Sales at 559-876-2170 or
email orders@familius.com.

Library of Congress Cataloging-in-Publication Data
2016939753   ISBN 9781942934721   eISBN 9781944822446

Printed in China

Book and jacket design by David Miles
Edited by Lindsay Sandberg and David Miles

10 9 8 7 6 5 4 3 2 1

First Edition

10 LITTLE MONSTERS visit CALIFORNIA

JESS SMART SMILEY

FAMILIUS

10 Little Monsters cannot wait
to visit the sunny Golden State.

10 Little Monsters head to the coast—
it's California they love the most!

Huntington Beach boasts ten miles of golden sand and some of the best surfing in the world. Most of its sand castles are monster-free, but caution is still warranted.

10 Little Monsters are happy to reach
the sand at the shore of Huntington Beach.
One Little Monster finds a sandcastle bare
and claims it for monsters everywhere.

First opening in 1916, the San Diego Zoo is home to over 3,500 animals, many of which are rare or endangered. Monsters are only allowed to visit.

9 Little Monsters at the San Diego Zoo wave to the tigers and a kangaroo.

One Little Monster is swept away.
"Go on without me—I'm here to stay."

8 Little Monsters trek through the night.
Yosemite's great in the dark and the light!

Yosemite National Park is roughly the same size as the state of Rhode Island. Night hikes are a popular pastime, but bring plenty of flashlights for the monsters in your party. Better yet, don't bring the monsters at all.

The sun rises warm and more hikes begin,
but one Little Monster settles right in.

7 Little Monsters slow to a trot.
"Death Valley is just a little too hot."

With a record temperature of 136 degrees, Death Valley is considered one of the world's hottest places. Ice cream is advised, but you'd better eat fast . . . or bring a soup spoon.

The Monsters retreat toward cooler fun . . .

. . . but one
monster stays to
soak up the sun.

Little Monsters visit the bay,
where Alcatraz Island invites them to stay.

The prison's exciting, but they
leave without crime . . .

. . . though one Little Monster
wants a little more time.

Alcatraz Island kept
some of the country's
most notorious criminals.
It's fascinating to visit,
but we recommend
finding other hotel
accommodations.

5 Little Monsters look all around
the Redwood Forest, from the sky to the ground.

They've lost a dear friend,
but it's time to move on,

Redwood trees
are the tallest
in the world.
They're stunning
to look at, but
you should
rethink those
treehouse plans.

4

Little Monsters want to play
with the sea creatures living at Monterey Bay.

3 Little Monsters start singing a song,
"The Golden Gate Bridge is sooooo long!"

"The traffic is also exciting,"
one states . . .

Over two billion cars have crossed the bridge since its opening in 1937. Only monsters find sitting in traffic exciting.

. . . and that Little Monster accelerates.

Rodeo Drive is lined with luxurious shops and restaurants. You might see a celebrity doing their shopping, but you probably won't see a monster.

2 Little Monsters, feeling alive, shop all along Rodeo Drive.

So many actors, so much to see—

"Let's make a movie starring you and me!"

1 Little Monster continues to roam
and finds that Lake Tahoe is better than home.

With the water and mountains and sun in the West . . .

Lake Tahoe is 1,645 feet deep, making it the second deepest lake in the United States. Don't try to cross it alone unless you can swim a dozen miles or are really, really tall.

. . . it's California these monsters love best!